MIGHTY MIKE
BUILDS A Ball Field

By Kelly Lynch   Illustrated by Casey Lynch

magic
wagon

visit us at www.abdopublishing.com

For Ray, who knows how to build almost anything – KL
For Mom and Dad – CL

Published by Magic Wagon, a division of the ABDO Group, 8000
West 78th Street, Edina, Minnesota 55439. Copyright © 2011 by
Abdo Consulting Group, Inc. International copyrights reserved in
all countries. All rights reserved. No part of this book may be
reproduced in any form without written permission from the publisher.

Looking Glass Library™ is a trademark and logo of Magic Wagon.

Printed in the United States of America, North Mankato, Minnesota.
092010
012011
 This book contains at least 10% recycled materials.

Written by Kelly Lynch
Illustrations by Casey Lynch
Edited by Stephanie Hedlund and Rochelle Baltzer
Cover and interior layout and design by Abbey Fitzgerald

Library of Congress Cataloging-in-Publication Data

Lynch, Kelly, 1976-
   Mighty Mike builds a ball field / by Kelly Lynch ; illustrated by Casey
Lynch.
        p. cm. -- (Mighty Mike)
   ISBN 978-1-61641-128-2
   [1. Building--Fiction. 2. Helpfulness--Fiction. 3. Community life--Fiction.] I.
Lynch, Casey, ill. II. Title.
   PZ7.L9848Mb 2011
   [E]--dc22
                                        2010016154

It was a sunny Saturday morning, and Mighty Mike was at his shop. He whistled as he greased his dozer, oiled his excavator, and detailed his dump truck. *What a beautiful morning*, he thought. It was spring, and the birds chirped as Mike worked.

Mighty Mike looked up from oiling and greasing just in time to see Kenny, Benny, Julie, and Janie climb onto his fence.

"Good morning," Mike greeted them. "What are you doing today?"

"Oh nothing," replied Kenny with a frown.

"Nothing?" asked Mighty Mike. "But it seems like the perfect day to do something!"

"We want to play ball," Benny piped in, "but there's no place to play."

"Yeah," added Julie. "There's not enough room at the park, and the school playground is too far away."

Hmmm, thought Mighty Mike as he rubbed his chin. Mike looked at the kids and said, "I might be able to help, but I'll have to do some thinking. Come back next Saturday."

Kenny, Benny, Julie, and Janie climbed down from the fence and started walking home. Mighty Mike continued greasing and oiling, but his mind was rumbling with ideas. He had decided to build them a ball field!

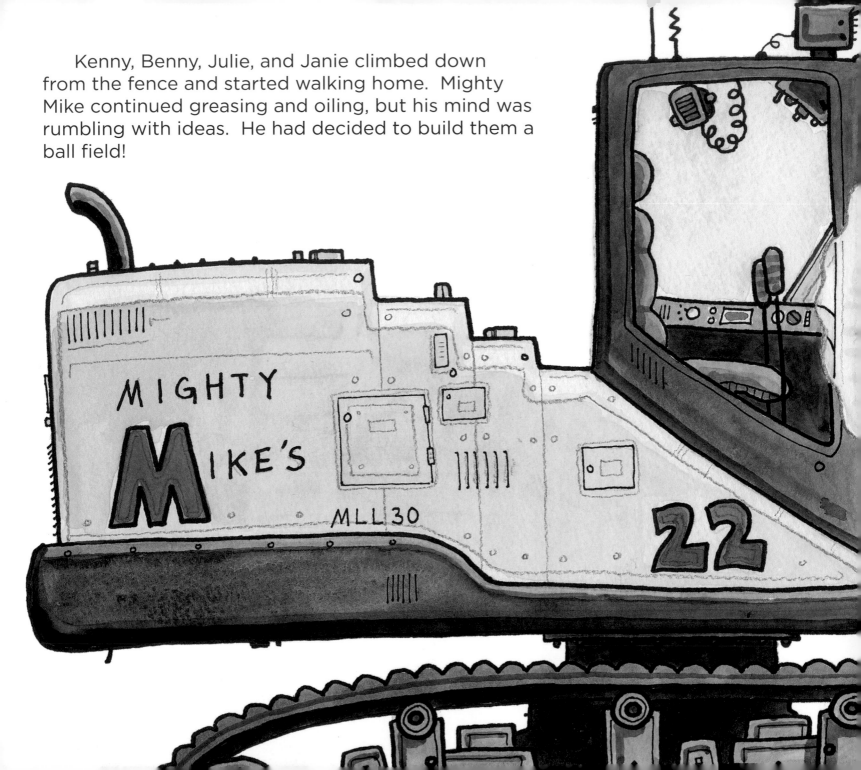

On Monday while the kids were at school, Mighty Mike started to work. He spent the day on his bulldozer, flattening all the lumps and bumps with the big blade until the ground was perfectly flat. At the end of the day, Mike was tired.

On Tuesday, Mighty Mike used a long tape measure to measure out the bases and home plate. Then with a shovel and a rake, Mike formed the pitcher's mound. *Perfect!* he thought. But, he was a little more tired than the day before.

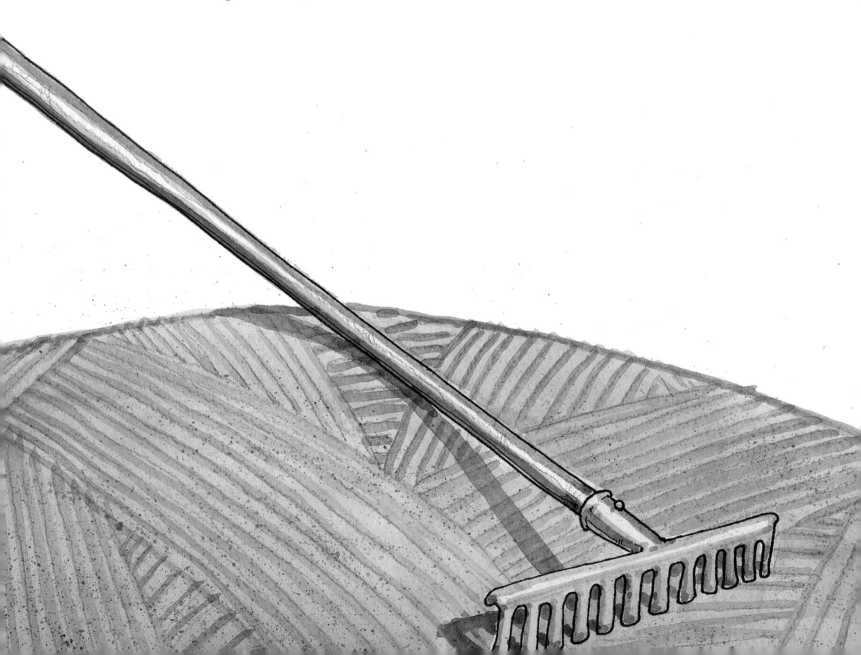

On Wednesday, Mighty Mike built a backstop out of steel poles and chain link behind home plate. *Now it's beginning to look like a ball field!* thought Mike. But when he finished, Mike was a little more tired than the day before.

On Thursday, Mighty Mike used a saw, a hammer, and nails to build the bleachers. It was hard work. He sawed, hammered, grunted, and sweated all day. And Mike was even more tired at the end of the day.

Friday was the hardest day. Mighty Mike rolled out roll after roll after roll of grassy sod to complete the ball field. By afternoon, he was very tired.

"Maybe I'm not that mighty," Mike said to Dozer. At the end of the day, the ball field was not done.

On Saturday morning, Mighty Mike woke up very glum. The ball field wasn't finished and he knew Kenny, Benny, Julie, and Janie would be coming soon. But Mighty Mike was too tired to finish the job. He didn't even get up when the kids arrived.

"What's wrong, Mighty Mike?" asked Kenny between breaths.
"Oh," replied Mike, "I was planning a surprise for you guys, but I didn't finish it."
"What is it?" asked Janie.
"I was building a new ball field for you," answered Mike.

"But it's not done," continued Mike.
"Well," said Kenny, "maybe we can help you finish it."
"Yeah!" piped in Julie. "We'll help you finish the ball field!"
And that is exactly what they did.

Kenny, Benny, Julie, and Janie pitched in. By Saturday afternoon, they were playing on their brand-new ball field. All it took was a little teamwork to get the job done.

"Work is a lot easier and more fun when you have help!" Mike declared when they finished.

So, if you're in Mighty Mike's neighborhood on a summer afternoon and you hear the crack of a bat, walk behind Mike's shop. You'll see Kenny, Benny, Julie, and Janie playing ball on the beautiful ball field that Mighty Mike built with a little help.

And if you are looking for Mighty Mike, he's sitting up in the bleachers cheering them on. Climb up next to him and enjoy the game!

Glossary

backstop - a screen or a fence that keeps a ball from leaving a ball field.

chain link - heavy steel wire woven into a diamond pattern.

excavator - a power-operated shovel.

sod - the upper part of soil that has grass and its roots.

What Would Mighty Mike Do?

• Why does Mighty Mike decide to build the ball field?

• How does Mighty Mike feel when he can't finish the ball field?

• What happens when Mighty Mike tells the children he can't finish?

• How does Mighty Mike feel when the ball field is finished?